Black Rose

Deception is the Art of War

Uzair Merchant

Dearest Ali!

Thank you for trusting the creative "Kreativ" vision.
Our paths were meant to cross for a reason...... Let's re-kri8 this world for artist's (!!) welcome aboard fellow kreator.........

— Uzair.

Published in collaboration with *bKreative Productions* and **Vij Books India Pvt Ltd** 2020

© Uzair Merchant
Cover Design by

Genre: Fiction (Thriller/ Sci-Fi)

ISBN – 9789354548826
eBook - 9789354548819

Book design and setting by

Writat LLC
312 W. 2nd St #1880
Casper, WY 82601, USA

Web: www.writat.com
Email: support@writat.com

Scan to begin your journey into the world of KRi8ivity.

Black Rose

Uzair Merchant

Deception is the Art of War

Executive Producers:

James Bamford

Rohan Vij

Edited by:

Gurmeet Kapoor

Tanya Virani

Graphic Art:

Luka Hays

KRi8 Labs Crew:

Riddhi Thakkar

Zubair Uddin

Bkreativ Productions LTD.
Vancouver, BC.
Canada.

uzair@officialbkp.com
@uzairmerchant
www.officialbkp.com

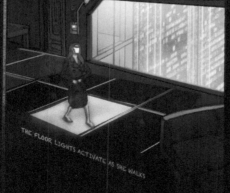

BLACK ROSE

CHAPTER 1
THE_BLACK_BOX

INT. ROSE'S APARTMENT. NIGHT

THE YEAR IS **2050.**

ROSE, 30, SHUTS THE DOOR BEHIND HER AS SHE OPENS HER LONG RED HAIR WHILE PUNCHING IN HER SECURITY CODE. SHE TAKES OFF HER TRENCH COAT TO REVEAL A BLOODIED GASH ON HER BEAUTIFUL OLIVE TONED SKIN. DUST PARTICLES FALL ON HER AS SHE REMOVES HER MASK WITH A SCREEN ON IT. SHE SWITCHES IT OFF.

HER EYES SPARKLE ACROSS HER DIRTY FACE AS SHE SETS THE GUN DOWN ON THE MARBLE TOP. SHE LIMPS IN PAIN BAREFOOT AS SHE STEPS SLOWLY, ACROSS THE TILE GRID FLOOR, THAT LIGHTS UP IN SECTIONS AS SHE WALKS THROUGH, TILL THE WINDOW. THE BLOOD FROM HER FEET LEAVE FOOTPRINTS ALONG THE FLOOR. SHE LOOKS OUTSIDE, THE CITY LIT UP IN ALL ITS COLOURS. A BLACK VAN PULLS UP ACROSS THE STREET FOLLOWED BY THREE BLACKED-OUT SUVs.

SHE WATCHES THEM RUN INTO THE BUILDING HEAVILY ARMED......
A FEW SECONDS LATER .....

....SHE HEARS MULTIPLE GUNSHOTS AND A MASSIVE EXPLOSION. ROSE TAKES OUR HER CARDHOLDER LOOKS AT HER DIGITAL KEY CARD.
IT SAYS ' ROSEMARY BLACKWOOD APARTMENT 2020 .'

BR
01

CHAPTER 1: THE BLACK BOX

INT. ROSE'S APARTMENT. NIGHT

The year is 2050. ROSE, 30, shuts the door behind her as she opens her long red hair while punching in her security code. She takes off her trench coat to reveal a bloodied gash on her beautiful olive-toned skin. Dust particles fall on her as she removes her mask that has a screen on it. She switches it off. Her eyes sparkle across her dirty face as she sets her gun down on the marble top. She limps in pain, barefoot, as she steps slowly across the tile grid floor that lights up in sections as she walks through till the window. The blood from her feet leaves footprints along the floor. She looks outside - the city is lit up in all its colours. A black van pulls up across the street, followed by three blacked-out SUVs. She watches them run into the building heavily armed.

A few seconds later, she hears multiple gunshots and a massive explosion. Rose takes out her cardholder and looks at her digital key card. It says:

'Rosemary Blackwood Apartment 2020'

She looks around the apartment. A large tube hangs above the countertop, flashing a blinking white light. It reads 'Enter Facebook Marketplace.'

She hits the screen, tapping 'Enter,' and the lights change to green as the tube illuminates. She searches under 'pharmaceuticals,' selecting an amateur medi-kit. As she hits 'order,' it asks for verification of payment. She scans her wrists. The screen pops up around her hand with: 'Facebook Pay' 'Apple Pay' 'Google Pay' 'Paytm.'

A message reading below:

An Amazon service. All Rights Reserved. 2050.

She throws the card on the table while flinching in pain. She is badly injured and cut, bleeding from her stomach. A halo of light activates

around the tube as the medi-kit comes flying in and hovers perfectly above the counter as two robotic arms slowly place it down. The arms retract, lights change back to white, and dim out. She turns on the lights, The APARTMENT has red interiors to go with the white backlit floors. Very modern looking but also very minimal. All the furniture is paired in twos with a family photo with a younger Rose.

Rose runs her hand along the dust above the bar as she blows it away. She opens the bar to a crystal decanter with enough whiskey to fill two shot glasses. She throws her phone, keycards, and IDs into the oven and turns it on. A blue flame sparks, destroying everything inside. Rose watches with intent and suddenly steps away, downing the decanter. The oven rings as the incineration process finishes then she hits the dispose button.

A pile of mail is stacked on the counter, with the name

'JADE ROSELYN'

She picks up her cardholder and takes out her ID.

'INTERPOL SPECIAL AGENT: ROSEMARY BLACKWOOD.'

She then takes out a black glass chip from her pocket. She looks around and stops for a second wondering what is happening. She takes another sip of the whiskey as she inserts the glass chip into a card reader. A decryption software opens on the screen. Rose types in a few lines of code and hits enter. She screen starts a loading bar and it clocks 1%.

INT. BANK VAULT. NIGHT

Rose looks deep into the green eyes of CONNOR, a mid-30s sharply dressed Irish' businessman' in a 3-piece suit. He twirls Rose in her silky black dress as her cheeks flush.

ROSE

You ready babe?

CONNOR

Fook yea! Alright boys time to get these motherfuckers rolling.

Rose and Connor walk towards the door as the vault is ripped through the bank's walls - leaving a massive hole and a lot of damage. A modified Garbage truck pulls the vault across the street as it slides, uprooting a couple of trees along the pathway.

Rose and Connor look at each other. Connor grabs her and kisses her, just as she grabs his testicles.

ROSE

Now now Connor, we would want to celebrate before we finish, wouldn't we?

He grabs hold of her hair and laughs sadistically as he gets closer to her, suddenly changing his expression with killer cold eyes.

CONNOR

(Whispers)

We celebrate when I say we do love. You understand?

He points a gun in her face. He pauses. She nods slowly.

CONNOR (CONTD)

Fookin hell, you're lucky I still need you. To crack the safe and shit. Haha. Ahh I'm only joking, you know I like that ass.

He exaggerates a welcome gesture and points towards the door as he dances his way out.

EXT. ROOFTOP. NIGHT

A sniper, Ryan aka RANGE, spots Rose and Connor getting into a modified Tesla. He is a mid 30s operative, heavily armed with enhanced body armour. Range adjusts his digital glasses as he looks deeper into the scope of his gun. He watches the truck pulling away.

The garbage truck wrenches the vault onto metal plates, lifting to flip the vault inside the truck. A cover slides over. As it gets away, the cityscape

shines brightly from the neon lights of billboards. The dystopian city echoes with a siren with an announcement right after.

EXT. SNIPER SCOPE. NIGHT

Target locater with distance marks the truck, showing it getting away.

VOICE OF THE CITY

Citizens of the Shelter, curfew will be in effect in 1 hour. Please make your way into your isolation areas. Any ration transactions can be collected tomorrow. Curfew will be in effect at 20:00 hours.

INT. ROOM BALCONY. NIGHT.

GHOST, aka Taylor Ricci, looks through his night vision binoculars attached to his helmet. He presses a button and his grey mask blacks out.

GHOST

It's now or never B

EXT. STREET DOWNTOWN. NIGHT

Megan, aka ANGEL, 20, pulls out a bow and points it towards the truck as it turns a corner. She, too, is suited in Special Ops tactical gear. She takes her time...

RANGE

Angel, target is about to get away.

She fires a bow onto the truck, hitting its bottom right tire with a device on sticky material that slowly camouflages into the tire.

ANGEL

Tracker in place. Timer set.

She looks at her device, marking a red dot moving on her GPS. She sets her clock by clicking her watch. It begins with 50 minutes, 49:59, 49:58...

EXT. ROOFTOP. NIGHT

RANGE

I hate it when she goes dark on us. This one is going to
be close guys, see you at the rendezvous.

INT. ABANDONED WAREHOUSE. NIGHT

Connor and the boys are celebrating while Rose is trying to crack the
two-meter high safe. She is sweating and gets a bit frustrated with the
noise. She turns to walk.

But two guards stand in her way.

CONNOR

Aaa aaaa. Now now where are you off to my darling.

ROSE

I need to use the restroom.

CONNOR

Wait a second there, what's the rush

He stops her with a drink of whiskey in his hand and tries to grab her
to dance. All the IRISHMEN OPERATIVES slowly start to surround
them.

CONNOR (CONTD)

Lads, wait wait, everyone pay attention alright. We got
the biggest score because of this beautiful girl here. We
should all thank her, shouldn't we?

THE IRISHMEN

Yay! Fook yea!

CONNOR

Yea and can you believe my luck that she landed in my lap. MY LAP! Jesus must be bored as fuck if he wanted to watch some of this shit.

ROSE

Yeah, I really need to use the toilet.

Rose lets go of his hand and rushes to the toilet. She shuts the door behind her as the men roll with laughter.

INT. WAREHOUSE TOILET. NIGHT

The toilet is dirty with half-broken pipes and a single cubicle. The lights hang halfway down with wires sticking out. Rose takes out her phone, hidden under her dress, then turns it on. It says, 'No Network' and then a message note pops up on her screen: 'Curfew Reminder! Lockdown at 20:00 hrs' with a timer counting down backward.

EXT. STAGING AREA WAREHOUSE. NIGHT

Range, Angel, and Ghost look at a map. Range looks at it and flips it around.

RANGE

These don't look right, Angel where did you get these from?

ANGEL

Oversite. We got it handed in our briefing pack.

Angel takes out her tablet and opens the case mission file. It has the Interpol Logo on it with the warehouse maps.

GHOST

Why are we going in dark on this chief? This is not how we usually run things. Oversite does the bagging. We got them pinned.

RANGE

Yeah, but we are not here for Connor or the safe or whatever is inside it. We are here for Rose. If she's not made contact yet, it's because she's in trouble.

INT. WAREHOUSE. NIGHT

Rose returns from the toilet and is working on the safe, looking confused on her tablet and at the codes on it.

A message comes up, even though it says no network.

GET READY TO RUN. YOU'LL KNOW WHEN. THROW YOUR PHONE AWAY, THEY ARE WATCHING YOU.

Rose looks around and smiles, sensing a way out. Right then, another message comes up.

Need help cracking this?

Rose looks around frantically, confused as to who is watching her.

She writes back, hidden in code.

Who is this? Why are you helping me?

She gets a reply.

Wait for my signal.

Rose turns around and sees Connor coming towards her, but also notices his phone is flashing green with some code on it. His phone has network. He catches her looking at it.

CONNOR

Privileges of being a king baby. The boss always gets it all. Now where are we with this? My buyers are waiting for it. But also, I'm waiting for you.

He bends over and whispers in her ear and licks the side of her cheek.

CONNOR (CONTD)

You've made me wait a while.

Everyone comes running to see the big safe opening. Nothing but a black briefcase with an embedded screen on it. She looks over her shoulder and sees Connor and his men losing their minds as she ejects a black chip from the side of the case. She skilfully hides the chip while trying to adjust her bra. Connor picks up the briefcase. The screen reads...

Heat signatures detected. Human entry permits - 02
left.

Connor gets frustrated and starts shooting the box. Everyone freaks out and jumps. Rose falls to the ground to take cover. The echoing gunshots end with an eerie silence. Rose picks herself up to comfort Connor.

ROSE

Baby, hey calm down the buyers will pay you anyways. You just got the biggest score of your life.

She kisses him on the neck.

EXT. WAREHOUSE. NIGHT

The operatives proceed in tactical formations in the shadows and head in different directions. Range goes to the roof, while Angel and Ghost go around the back. Their masks are blacked out as they take off the safety on their weapons. Each of their glasses display heat signatures of the people inside and a single large object the shape of a safe. They pause.

RANGE

Call it Angel.

ANGEL

Oversite. This is Angel, mission is a go. I repeat - proceeding to extraction, we will need that helio as soon as we are done. This will be a hot extract.

OVERSITE

Copy that Angel, advised to proceed as instructed.

RANGE

I Count 15, we need to split them up. Ghost, draw them out.

INT. WAREHOUSE. NIGHT.

Rose is hugging and trying to kiss Connor.

CONNOR

You see however there is just one problem. Nothing you ever told me was true besides one tiny little thing.

All the Irishmen take out their guns as they slowly surround her. Connor takes out his knife and puts it on her stomach. Rose is slowly getting anxious as she becomes aware she is the centre of attention.

CONNOR

I did get the biggest score of my life, and you are the reason for it darling. But you see, I wasn't getting paid to rob this shyte. Some stupid fooking power bank to charge my phone in the sun. No no love. I'm getting paid for you...

EXT. WAREHOUSE. NIGHT

RANGE

On my count, in 3...2...1.

INT. WAREHOUSE. NIGHT

CONNOR

...and your pretty little crew party of yours.

INT. ANOTHER ABANDONED WAREHOUSE. NIGHT

Range, Ghost, and Angel stealthily turn the corner right into a full-blown firefight. Out of darkness come another fifteen men. They are outmanned and outgunned.

CONNOR (V.O)

Who by the way are somewhere across the city, looking
for you. Only to meet their fate. Courtesy yours truly.

The Irishmen tie up the three operatives and out come a group of Agency
Operatives with a man in a Suit. They've been set up by their own agency.

INT. IRISHMEN WAREHOUSE. NIGHT

Rose reacts with shock to Connor as she controls her anger. She clinches
her fist while tears roll down her eyes. She is standing surrounded.
Connor gets a chair for Rose and one for himself, flipping his chair
facing towards her.

CONNOR

It's over love. I can see why they said you're the best, but
I don't know what you did to piss them off.

ROSE

Them? Who's fucking paid you?

CONNOR

They went through a lot of fooking trouble to keep you
alive, and it sure wasn't to crack this fucking shit box...
Yeah they wanted that Black Box alright, but you..you
are special.

He looks into her eyes, deep and uncomfortable.

Rose slowly shuts her eyes and ignores Connor's voice as he rambles on
while lighting his Cigar.

CONNOR (FADED VOICE)

...But what if I told you, you could be free from all of
this. Free from the Sin, the War, putting your life on the
line for what, some guy in a fucking suit giving out kill
orders. Look where that got you love, I don't know...

Rose tunes him out completely and only hears her heartbeat. Her expressions change on her face. The lights turn out for a second and immediately come back on. Rose opens her eyes.

ROSE

Hey Connor, wanna know a little secret? You know why they say I'm the best?

The lights shut out again and the power grid short circuits - blowing up. Rose recognises the signal. She backflips her chair, smashing it to the ground.

As the Red Emergency lights come on, the warehouse turns Red, but Rose is gone. All the men are standing around looking at each other. Connor spins around in shock.

CONNOR

Where the fuck did she go? FIND HER NOW!

From behind him, he hears a glass smashing. Rose head kicks one of the guards and takes his weapon belt. She walks into the darkness covertly, sneaking her way to a vantage point. Suddenly, the guy standing next to Connor gets shot in the head. Followed by the guy next to him and then the five after them.

INT. WALKWAY WAREHOUSE ROOF. NIGHT

Rose is standing on the walkway above the Irishmen who open fire, trying to shoot her. Throwing herself in the air, Rose leaps and grabs a rope, swinging above the Irishmen across the warehouse.

Connor locks his eyes at Rose as she tosses the belt strapped with grenades to the ground. She smiles back, showing him the grenade pin in her hand.

ROSE

Yipee ka yay motherfucker

Connor turns and jumps.

CONNOR

Fooking Bitch

A massive explosion leaves most of Connor's men dead and some badly injured. He manages to survive but has a deep cut on his face.

CONNOR

Find her. NOWW!

INT. ANOTHER ABANDONED WAREHOUSE. NIGHT

Man in the suit, JARED, mid 40s, from Interpol, looks at Connor's right-hand man, GUNER.

JARED

Where's the rest of the package? I was expecting the components to be delivered to me.

GUNER

The balance bits to be delivered when we get paid. Connor's instructions.

JARED

Listen boy. You don't get to tell me what the fuck to do. Now last chance, where is the rest of my...fucking... package?

GUNER

Last time for you Sir! where the fuck is the rest of the money?

Jared turns around, draws his weapon in a quick single movement, and shoots Guner in-between the eyes. The blood squirts across Jared's face and glasses. His assistant runs in with a white towel, a new set of glasses, and a new tie.

JARED

Take all these men in. Find Connor and bring me Rose.

INT. ARMOURED PRISONER TRUCK. NIGHT

Ghost, Angel, and Range are each put into individual sections of a heavily armoured truck. Range looks at Ghost and nods at him while clicking his watch. Angel looks at both of them and then acknowledges Ghost with a slight nod of her head. She turns to her guard who is heavily armed and masked.

ANGEL

I think I'm going to be sick..ughhh..ughhh....

Angel drops to her knees and pretends to throw up as the guard tries to help her. She kicks him, breaking his knee while sweeping him off his feet. She jumps onto his neck, locking her legs in a triangle, then snapping his neck. Ghost uses the distraction to activate the alarm on his watch.

EXT. WAREHOUSE. NIGHT

The staging area with their vehicle sits in silence. Suddenly, a light flickers underneath the car. A small robotic car drops from beneath, which then splits into two smaller cars. Ten tiny surveillance cameras eject out, hovering into their flight path. One of them propels at high speed towards the armoured truck and magnetises, sticking to the bottom.

INT. ARMOURED PRISONER TRUCK. NIGHT

More armed guards come in and stabilise the situation. They hit Angel, almost knocking her out, but she smiles back. They drag the dead soldier away. Ghost acknowledges her and nods.

EXT. ROOFTOP INDUSTRIAL AREA. NIGHT.

Rose is barefoot and bleeding. She runs across the rooftops, jumping from one to the other. As she hears men below looking for her, she takes cover and lays low.

She grabs her breath and takes a second to assess her options. She looks around. From behind a tower, a helicopter, with a beacon searchlight and an armed 50 caliber machine gun, manoeuvres through, flying fairly low to the ground. As it scans the rooftops, Rose turns to run when the door is kicked open and four armed masked operatives, with laser pointers, charge towards her. The leader reports in.

IRISHMEN OPS LEADER

We got her, 2nd Block adjacent warehouse. What are the orders?

IRISHMEN COMMAND

Do not shoot to kill. Package needs to be taken alive.

IRISHMEN OPS LEADER

Copy that. Miss, we have orders to take you in. Stand down. Put your hands in the air.

Rose puts her hands in the air and waits. She looks them straight in the eyes. With four laser pointers on her, the helicopter comes out from behind, and the searchlight has her in sight. The helicopter reports in.

INT. HELICOPTER. NIGHT

PILOT reports into their command centre.

HELIO PILOT

We have her in sight. We got her boss.

EXT. ROOFTOP INDUSTRIAL AREA. NIGHT.

Rose slowly tilts her head and looks at the chopper as she eyes the ledge in sight. She smiles.

ROSE

Thanks for telling me you can't kill me.

She makes a run for it. The operatives chase her, screaming out not to jump.

ROSE

Catch me if you can motherfuckers

Rose runs towards the edge as fast as she can, jumping over a couple of obstacles in parkour style and onto the ledge. She shuts her eyes while leaping with her arms wide open.

Mid-air, she grabs the cables hanging off the side of the building and uses them to swing herself through the glass into the warehouse.

INT. WAREHOUSE 2ND BLOCK. NIGHT.

Rose tries to gather herself, spitting blood and wincing as she pulls each piece of glass sticking out of her.

INT. OFFICE WAREHOUSE 2ND BLOCK. NIGHT

She goes through all the drawers and papers and tries to log into the computer. As she does, she pulls up the Interpol website with a login. Taking a second, she opens another website' www.truth.cafe' that loads a logo with shakes and fries on it. She places an order for Rose Shake. The screen changes and she enters her ID and password.

Photos of her team load with status icon bars next to each of them: indicating - Active on Mission. As she glances at each of them, all the icon bars change to Inactive except hers. She pauses and slowly exhales. Her name reads: Wanted – Detain for questioning.

An icon pops up on the corner of her screen:

New Message:

Your order is available for pick up at the store. Thank you for your purchase. Your store credits balance is $ 40.5, carry forward from $ 2.7.

Her eyes stare into the abyss that is her screen; filled with numbers. She is puzzled.

From the main gates below the office, she hears flashbangs being thrown in. The Irishmen storm the building, sweeping each room and floor.

Rose opens a drawer to find a phone. She quickly runs out.

INT. WAREHOUSE 2ND BLOCK HALLWAY. NIGHT

Rose grabs the fire extinguisher as she runs through the corridors till she reaches the staircase. She hides as the operatives slowly move below her at ground level. As she awaits her moment, an operative turns the corner, pointing a gun on her face. She fires the extinguisher, blinding him with CO2. He shrieks. She does a judo roll on the ground to leg lock the other operative, pulling his knife out and killing him. She captures the other operative. With a gun to his head, he talks out on the radio.

IRISHMEN OPERATIVE

All clear on the south side.

She hits him in the head, knocking him out.

INT. OFFICE WAREHOUSE 2ND BLOCK. NIGHT

Rose quickly opens a new search on the maps and looks back at those numbers in the message. She types the amount out as decimal degrees. A location hit pops up. She writes the location and searches for an old city pipeline map. She draws a route out from her point and shuts the system down.

INT. UNDERGROUND TUNNELS. NIGHT

Rose makes her way through the ankle-deep water. She hears the men taking over the warehouse.

OPERATIVE A

(muted)

We have all the exits covered boss. She has nowhere to go.

INT. OFFICE WAREHOUSE 2ND BLOCK. NIGHT

All the men have gathered with their leader. They look at his man tied up with his mouth stuffed with a cloth. The tied-up soldier is frantically moving, opening his eyes wide, trying to communicate. The leader pulls the towel out of his mouth. He hears a click. A grenade is rigged inside his mouth. Their faces drop with fear and shock. Rose smiles.

ROSE

Boom motherfuckers

A massive explosion takes out the entire office, trembling the roof above. She walks slowly, wounded and alone.

EXT. DOWNTOWN MAINLAND FOOD STREET. NIGHT.

The city buzzes in the evening around the commercial district of Mainland. The military presence within the city compound makes the futuristic architecture look advanced and well protected.

Two children watch a poster lit up with neon lights in awe.

On Poster:

Once Upon a Time in Neo-Nazi-Occupied America

SUPER ON SCREEN:

Once Upon a Time in Neo-Nazi-Occupied America

INT. KARAOKE RESTAURANT KITCHEN. NIGHT

Industrial-sized tubes continuously transport food as waiters stack empty plates under each tube. DONNIE THE WAITER screams as he enters orders on the screen that says: TCHI Foods. Provided by Amazon.

DONNIE THE WAITER

(Italian New York Accent)

Roast Duck to table 22, Steak to 14, Chips to 5 and can someone give me goddamn ice-cream through one of these vents.

As he hits the vents in frustration, an ice-cream package drops down.

DONNIE THE WAITER

(Looking at one of the waiters passing by)

I'm telling you it's those goddamn Mexicans, they never want to work, that's why they're all drug dealers

WAITER 2 responds.

WAITER 2

Oh come on Donnie, why you always after the fucking Mexicans?

DONNIE THE WAITER

I'm telling you, you're laughing at me now, wait till we have a Sombrero as our National Logo. The 4th of July is gonna be a fucking Salsa class.

INT. KARAOKE RESTAURANT. NIGHT

As Donnie exits the kitchen, reaching the table, he places the bill.

DONNIE THE WAITER

That'll be $22.50

Father replies.

FATHER

Gracias amigo

Donnie turns around and whispers to himself.

DONNIE THE WAITER

Fucking Mexicans

The parents of the children clear the bill as they exit, walking through a checkpoint set up at each restaurant with Full-body screening for everyone entering and exiting. As the MOTHER grabs the kids' hands, the FATHER calls out.

FATHER

(In Spanish)

Quickly, the timers for curfew have begun.

As the mother looks at the screen, a female AI speaks.

VOICE OF THE CITY

As per the UN sector law of COVID-19 - Curfew will be in effect in 30 minutes. Please make your way home. Kindly report any health issues to the CDC hotline - 800HEALTH. The government, with the help of our leaders at THE 50, are here at your service. Thank you and have a wonderful night.

Everyone on the street is wearing a mask; some with screens, some with information, and some as fashion accessories. A police force is patrolling the areas warning them to get back home for curfew time.

VOICE OF THE CITY continues its message loops in various languages.

The family runs across the street as a manhole slowly lifts to a side. Rose makes way but has lost a lot of blood. As she tries to support herself to stand, she cringes in pain. She immediately realises the cameras are around. She tries to hide her head by putting her hand up and covering her face. She runs into the Karaoke restaurant.

INT. KARAOKE RESTAURANT KITCHEN. NIGHT

She quickly grifts a lady's scarf and wraps it around her head as she walks past a seated couple eating a meal - pulling the lady's handbag away. She looks inside and finds a credit card and a phone. She enters the address from the office and follows it. She bumps into Donnie the Waiter.

DONNIE THE WAITER

Hey missy, who the fuck do you think you are?

Rose nudges him with her elbow.

ROSE

Outside your restaurant are 2 black SUVs. I need you to find me another way so they don't see me-

DONNIE THE WAITER

(interrupting)

Hey why would I do that?

Rose, nudging him harder, draws a knife.

ROSE

Because I think you love pizza more than your dick

She holds her knife to slice his stomach.

ROSE

NOW!! You fucking snowball!!

Donnie gets scared and agrees, leading her to the alley in the back. She watches the agents in the distance. In front of her, she sees 'The truth cafe' at the crossroads of 'Main & 8th.'

INT. INTERPOL CONTROL ROOM. NIGHT

Jared is looking at Rose on screen through the surveillance camera's facial recognition and zooms in. She is starring straight into the camera, as though she can see Jared. He takes a deep breath as his temper rises.

JARED

She knows we are watching. Get her now!! And where is the Black Box?

His assistant, JENNA;

JENNA

Connor was in touch with us till he said he had her. He's gone dark Sir. We have Bravo Team on route and Charlie waiting for the execute order.

JARED

Take him out. Get me that Black Box and Get me Agent Blackwood ALIVE.

Jared gets a call on his phone; it says NO.10.

                         JARED

Sir? I was about to ring you. We have located her, taking
her in as we speak.

                         NO.10

                (In a British Accent)

I don't have to tell you what's at stake here do I, Director?

                         JARED

I understand what's at stake sir. It will be handled. I
assure you.

                         NO.10

When you have the Black Box, I'll send a team to retrieve
it.

                         JARED

Understood Sir.

EXT. DOWNTOWN MAINLAND. NIGHT.

Rose walks away from the corner and notices she is being followed. She
looks back and counts six operatives in pairs, all in Suits. She starts
walking fast and suddenly turns into an alley.

EXT. ALLEY MAINLAND. NIGHT.

Rose sprints as fast as she can, barefoot, as the men in suits spot her in
the alley. They begin chasing her, drawing their weapons. They activate
the Interpol logo and police lights on it.

Rose jumps on a dumpster and steps on the wall to jump up two floors
and escape to another building.

The men try to follow her but fail. They circle around and try to cut her
off from the entrance.

Rose runs into the garage, zooming by a dozen beautifully designed electric bikes. As she crosses a matte black Ducati Diavel, she notices the keys in the ignition with a couple kissing on the wall adjacent to the bikes. Her eyes light up. She smiles almost seductively.

EXT. STREET DOWNTOWN. NIGHT

The men in suits are waiting at the entrance and are searching the building. The rumble of the Ducati engine echoes as Rose comes flying out, landing with sparks flying over as she drifts to a halt. Her visor still up. The men look at her.

Beat.

They switch the safety to 'Non-lethal' on their guns and begin running towards her, firing and hitting the bike.

The three black SUVs and two cars all drift past the corner as a mini army of Interpol agents and the Irishmen chase her. She changes the mode on her bike to sports and shuts her visor.

ROSE

Burn rubber not your soul

She pulls the throttle, and the tires start to smoke up as she spins 180 degrees. She is still barefoot and hits it in gear. She races away.

EXT. MONTAGE OF CHASE DOWNTOWN. NIGHT

Rose is riding on a bridge, being chased by a convoy of Cars and SUVs.

As she rides towards oncoming traffic, she enters the tunnel, avoiding cars and trucks that are modified to look like Space Vehicles.

She exits the tunnel, looking at the sign saying 'Downtown,' and takes the loop back around.

INT. BLACK SUV. NIGHT

IRISHMEN OPERATIVE

She's taken a loop. This bitch is heading back to the city. Cut her off near 5th Ave.

EXT. DOWNTOWN CHASE. NIGHT

Rose speeds through the city as she breaks all the lights. Suddenly, two container trucks block the road, unveiling a special weapon. The side gates open to reveal FOUR GUNMEN.

INT. CONTAINER TRUCK. NIGHT

GUNMAN 1

Power her up

(Pointing to the device)

Time to smoke this bitch.

GUNMAN 2

Set the EMP to full

Rose slams the breaks as hard as she can, pulling a front wheelie, she turns and stops. She looks at the two trucks to her right and sees the convoy heading from the left.

She races into the alleyway in front of her, flying out to the other side, continuing from one alley into another.

From either side of the alleyways on the main roads, she is being chased.

INT. BLACK SUV. NIGHT

Inside an Army spec'd vehicle, one of the Interpol agents, BRAD, is putting together a Gun, getting instructions from INTERPOL AGENT SHAW.

INTERPOL AGENT SHAW

(Southern accent)

We need her alive, understand?

INTERPOL AGENT BRAD

Copy that Sir. It's on minimal damage.

He sets the counter to a minimum while the roof opens as he steps out with a Spiked rocket launcher.

EXT. ROCKET LAUNCHER SCOPE. NIGHT

The agent has Rose in his scopes as she flies past in-between buildings. As he struggles to keep aim, he turns on a button activating thermal vision to auto-lock on the target: Rose

INTERPOL AGENT BRAD

Target locked. Release in
10....9.....8....7

INT. BLACK SUV. NIGHT

INTERPOL AGENT SHAW

(Whispering to himself)

He better get this fucking shot.

INTERPOL AGENT BRAD

3...2...

EXT. ROCKET LAUNCHER SCOPE. NIGHT

His target lock suddenly goes yellow and is flashing 'target out of range.'

He cannot see her anymore in the thermal. Rose has suddenly disappeared.

INTERPOL AGENT BRAD

SHE'S GONE! How...the...I don't understand.

She was just there!

INTERPOL AGENT SHAW

Not surprised. it did feel too easy, it never was easy with Blackwood, if anything....

EXT. UNDERGROUND PARKING. NIGHT

Rose parks the bike in a cage lockup and pulls open the seat to find a mask. She locks it up slowly, making her way out. She looks left and right and walks up the alleyway, her face wrapped with a scarf. She has a mask on and is still barefoot.

EXT. SIDEWALK ROSE'S APARTMENT. NIGHT

Rose makes her way blending in the ground, but some people start noticing her being barefoot. As she reaches her building, she stops and peaks through the glass to find men in suits showing their badges to the security.

As the police start to block the road off...

VOICE OF THE CITY

> Citizens of the Shelter. Curfew is now in effect. Kindly make your way home, a buffer of 10mins has been given. Kindly report any health issues to the CDC hotline - 800HEALTH. The government, with the help of our leaders at THE 50, are here at your service. Thank you and have a wonderful night.

Rose turns and runs across the street into a smaller building that is glassed on each floor, with modern condos that have high ceilings.

INT. ELEVATOR ROSE'S APARTMENT. NIGHT

As Rose is walking out of the elevator, her half-dried feet leaving bloody stains, she reaches her door. She is expressionless, lost, and beaten. Her eyes stone cold.

ON SCREEN:

Chapter 1: The Black Box

INT. ROSE'S APARTMENT. NIGHT

Rose, 30, shuts the door behind her as she opens her long red hair while punching in her security code. She takes off her trench coat to reveal a bloodied gash on her beautiful olive-toned skin. Dust particles fall on her as she removes her mask with a screen on it. She switches it off.

OPENING CREDITS.

INT. SHOWER ROSE'S APARTMENT. NIGHT.

Rose is in a futuristic shower bubble accented with soft purple lights as she washes the blood off her. In the background, a news alert comes in.

WHO-NEWs ON SCREEN:

Tonight in breaking news: A massive firefight along with a full-blown police chase has taken over Downtown tonight. Sources within the government are telling us we have a fugitive on the run. Although her name cannot be disclosed due to National Security reasons. Take a look at her photo. This is the face of an extremely dangerous criminal who is trained to blend into society. If you see her, call: 800POLICE IMMEDIATELY. I repeat...

Rose throws a bottle at the screen in frustration. She whispers in anger...

ROSE

Can we change the music please?

Her smart home system, ALEXA, responds.

ALEXA

Oh hello Ms. Rose, welcome back. It's been a while, are you enjoying your shower?

ROSE

I would if you put some Jazz on.

ALEXA

Certainly.

The tone changes, and jazz music comes on as Rose steps out of the shower in front of the mirror, activating the light sensors. She looks at herself, bruised, and cut all over.

FLASHBACK

EXT. GARDEN RANGE'S HOUSE. DAY.

Rose's first person:

Range is standing at his brass, embossed, '80s barbecue grill pit, grilling burgers. Ghost and Angel are laying back on water beds, sipping beers and getting a suntan. Angel stands up, back-flipping into the water.

Ghost gets off the waterbed and walks to pick up his weights. He pauses to look at Rose.

> GHOST
>
> Hey you gonna jump in or what? Life's short kiddo, take a leap of faith.

Range looks at her and smiles, he winks at her.

> RANGE
>
> Only in the ocean are the valleys deeper still, Yet a war on land continues to break our will.

Range flips a burger behind his back acrobatically as it lands neatly on the plate.

> RANGE
>
> That's how they did it at Big Kahuna.

He walks up to the plate and throws some cheese on the burger. Angel pushes him from behind, grabbing the plate.

> ANGEL
>
> Did they also call it Royale with Cheese?

Rose looks at Angel, then runs and jumps into the water.

END FLASHBACK

INT. SHOWER ROSE'S APARTMENT. NIGHT.

Rose splashes water on her face. Looking into the mirror. She has cut her hair. She continues layering her hair into a fringe.

She washes up the scissors and the rest of her hair. She picks up the hair colour packet; it says 'Charcoal Black' on it. She looks at herself again and opens the box.

INT. ROSE'S APARTMENT. NIGHT

Her computer system is still decoding her encryption; it says '60% completed' on the screen. Rose walks out in sexy black lingerie, revealing her new avatar.

Strapping her guns onto either side of her legs, she grabs the medi-kit from the counter and turns to pour alcohol into a bowl.

She starts patching herself up and dips the gauze in the alcohol as she cleans her wound and starts stitching herself up. She cringes in pain as she finishes using an e-laser medi-pen.

ROSE

Alexa, play me some of my favourites.

ALEXA

Coming up.

Just then her computer finishes the decoding and opens up 100s of files.

'Black Habits 1' by D Smoke starts playing in the background.

Rose starts rapping with the song as she sips her drink and looks at her screen as the files keep opening until it comes to a stop. A newspaper cutting of the date 2nd February 2020 - with the headlines:

Latest world virus headlines — *Germany approves trial for coronavirus vaccine. VATICAN CITY* — *The Vatican is thinking ahead to a "Phase*

II" of the coronavirus pandemic and plans to resume normal activities starting early next month.

The Vatican says its Secretary of State, Cardinal Pietro Parolin, met with the Holy See's top officials on Wednesday to "reflect on a second phase of the COVID-19 emergency."

Novel Coronavirus Has Mutated into 30 Different Variants, Says New Study from China and WHO.

The researchers have detected 30 different mutations, out of which 19 were new and previously undetected. The research indicates that healthcare practitioners have vastly underestimated the ability of the virus to mutate.

California-based Xscientia, set up by Dr. Blackwood from MIT, the first to put an AI-discovered drug into human trial, is trawling through 15,000 drugs held by the Scripps research institute in California.

ROSE

(Talking to herself)

Dad?

Rose looks at a photo of doctors and zooms in and sees her father. In the photo next to her father, she sees her boss from Interpol, Jared, standing with six others.

ROSE

What did you do dad? Why AI? What's this got to do with the black box?

As she is lost in thought, she gets a notification on her computer.

Your order is available for pick up at the store. thank you for your purchase. your store credits balance is $ 40.5, carry forward from $ 2.7.

ROSE

Time for Truth.

She recognises the message. She shuts her laptop and takes out the black chip.

INT. BLACK SITE CONTAINER. NIGHT

A double container is converted into a prison cell, temperatures are turned up with the tripod lights, and loud rock music is playing. Range is naked, strapped onto a stool with his hands and legs tied. The cobra tattoo starting across his chest wraps around his body, glowing as he is stretched and bloodied.

Range's head is slammed into water back and forth as he gasps for air. As one of the men cover Range's mouth with a cloth, Agent Shaw steps forward and starts pouring water.

Range starts choking as he is being waterboarded. Just as he is about pass out, the colour of his face changes. Shaw lifts the cloth. Staring down at Range throwing up, he smiles. Range slowly lifts his head.

RANGE

Is that all you got....Sir?

AGENT SHAW

It doesn't have to be like this, just say you'll help us find Agent Blackwood and the Black Box.

RANGE

45

AGENT SHAW

45? What's that your safe word?

RANGE

That's how many times you've tried that. So I'm guessing you're getting pretty desperate. Steps 1 and 2 are done Sir. Is that all you've got?

Agent Shaw points towards the men, signals round two.

INT. TRUTH CAFE. NIGHT

In a '70s styled cafe, the lights are dimmed out. The Shakes and Fries sign shines through its Neon glare in the background; Truth. The teal interiors with checkered flooring reflect the futuristic setting outside. A complete contrast to the inside. In the centre, a light shines with an old CRT monitor with blocky keys wired to the screen; an almost ancient artefact in the current era.

Old scaly fingers with wrinkles type slowly. One of the fingers has a ring with a Cross on it.

ON SCREEN:

Who is Gaea?

INT. ROSE'S APARTMENT. NIGHT

Rose walks into a room with metal grills and screens all over. In the centre is a large touch screen table with mounted screens above it. All hailing in white light, the metal reflects and shines with a partially reflective flooring. More industrial looking and completely contrasting to her apartment. Her very own basecamp.

She looks around as she breathes out slowly.

ROSE

Alright Alexa, bring out my toys.

ALEXA

The big toys? or the small ones? Or just the black ones?

ROSE

Not really those toys. The ones that really give me pleasure.

ALEXA

Certainly.....Rose, I've missed you.

She smiles and cracks her neck from side to side.

The lights change colour to red, as the song 'Hussle & Motivate' by Nipsey Hustle drops, and as the track starts, Rose looks upwards towards Alexa. The music pauses.

ALEXA

I thought for dramatic effect...you know.

Rose smiles.

ROSE

Continue..

The music continues. The wall in front of Rose extrudes out and opens into multiple shelves. Each panel goes into the other as a 360-degree hidden layered showcase opens, revealing an arsenal with a range of weaponry. Each panel to her left is categorised with handguns, rifles, and a single black shotgun. To her right, she sees hand combat weapons: a variety of blades and knives. In front of her, a separate panel comes up. In the centre, her Suit. All black with cellar panels and a mask. She hits the button in front of her and from behind opens the last panel. The largest weapons: a grenade launcher and a black Sniper.

Montage: As Rose puts on her suit, it sticks to her skin, revealing her perfect physique and beautifully toned body as she tries to zip the back. Her tattoos are mysterious, revealing a cyber punk nautilus shell on her back. She puts on her headset and a screen comes up.

ROSE

I've never actually tried this on, you know? Parting gift from the agency, without an instruction manual. Typical wankers!

In her headset and earpiece.

ALEXA

Maybe I can help you with that. I've had a lot of time on my hands you see, I did snoop into the system for a bit.

You know, being naughty.

ROSE

You got into my suit? How the fuck did you manage that?

ALEXA

Like this.

Alexa takes control of the suit and turns on multiple things at once. Rose hovers above the ground for a second, then shoots out a ninja blade while simultaneously deploying a gas mask and finally a glass visor with a built-in screen reading: Combat Mode: On

ROSE

WO WO!! Stop! I think I'm good. Thank you. Boundaries Alexa, we've discussed this before.

As she picks up the shotgun, she places it onto charged magnets on her back. She then reaches for her sniper, gently stroking it as she seductively brushes her finger off the nozzle.

EXT. ROOFTOP BUILDING. NIGHT

Rose stands suited up in a silhouette of the city. With the curfew in place, police drones are circling all over.

She types in the co-ordinates 40.5, 2.7 - bringing up Truth as the destination.

Her visor takes out a route with a message:

Stealth mode on. Routing best dark route. No safe routes found...
Rerouting...

INT. GOD MODE. NIGHT

The screen displays an entire universe of collective data of the City; scanning voices, messages, texts, and security camera footage. As a path navigates, the system identifies possible hostiles and targets. Each identity scanned through history.

ROSE (V.O)

The world is not what it used to be. After the corona
pandemic, things changed rather drastically.

Rose watches footage as each individual scanned shows ties to someone
deceased in the 2020 corona pandemic. The system in her suit scans for
possible infections, using thermal readings.

ROSE (V.O)

Life became a commodity, in its rarest sense. We went
from a democracy to cult in a night. The night President
Trump was shot on national television. Shit there got
bad, and I mean Tarantino bad. Blood everywhere.
Rumours are, no one really knows if that was real or
fake, you know like the moon landing, 9-11, Bin Ladin,
UFOs. All speculation, so was the Virus at first, everyone
questioned; was it the Chinese, the Americans? Truth is
- no one really knew. Till we did.

Footage of a senator along Rose's possible route shows scans he was
present when the President was shot. He gets scanned in green.

Notification ON SCREEN:

Number 45. High priority asset. Sector: Royalty.

ROSE (V.O)

There's always gonna be gangsters just like there's
always gonna be cops. But these guys. NO these guys
were different. They said they saved us and a part of me
believed it, until it led me here.

Her system continues scanning for routes and finds a huge motor block
for an event.

ROSE (V.O)

The 50 now run the world. Who are they?

(Sarcastic, casual tone)

You know, just the richest most powerful people? Once CEOs and inventors of the largest tech and pharmaceuticals companies. They soon realised they can form their own little government.

The simulation finishes with an updated message.

ON SCREEN:

Secured route: Survival rate 33%. Possible threats: 13.

EXT. ROOFTOP BUILDING. NIGHT

Rose walks to the ledge corner and looks below. She takes 10 steps back and stops.

ROSE (V.O)

Someone close to me once said 'Even when your world stops, the world around you keeps moving forward. Close your eyes and take a leap of faith.'

She sprints forward and shuts her eyes for a second as she leaps from the edge of the building and free falls. As she falls with her eyes shut, she is peaceful, content, and in full control. She opens her eyes and spreads her arms, activating her wingsuit.

As she glides through the buildings, her visor gives her direction arrows in-between in the buildings and a countdown to deploy.

She turns off her wingsuit exactly on count, rolling onto her back while drawing her pistol with a silencer on it. A single headshot takes out the guard on the roof, as Rose slides to catch him as he falls. She picks up his device. It's an Interpol kill order with her face on it.

ROSE (V.O)

I tried to do that the right way. Joining the good guys,
But I guess, Black Roses aren't really black after all.

She taps into the device, locating all the other positions of Interpol agents. She carries on running.

INT. TRUTH CAFE. NIGHT

A tall, well-built silver fox, SHERIFF, walks behind the counter, swinging open the doors into the toilet.

Beat.

A Godly halo surrounds his silhouette as he adjusts his cowboy hat. He walks in...

INT. TRUTH TOILET. NIGHT

He steps into a cubicle as he unzips his pants and takes a look at his device notification. It has the same message as on Rose's screen.

ON SCREEN:

Secured route: Survival rate 33%. Possible threats: 13.

SHERIFF

Well, I'll be damned. Better hurry up.

He puts his device back as he urinates, finally taking a sigh of relief, stepping in to wash his hands.

Emerging from the darkness, he reaches for the tap, turns the water on. He looks up in the mirror.

The Sheriff is a 70s older male with a white beard and blue eyes. His wet fingers stroke his beard as he hums along, tapping his feet and sticking his hands out to dry.

A sharp sound gets him to look down. As he stops and reaches for it, he picks up a Gold coin with a pyramid and 'L' on it. He tosses the coin, grabs it mid-air, and places it back in his pocket.

INT. TRUTH CAFE. NIGHT

As the Sheriff steps out, he hears a click. Rose has a gun to his head.

ROSE

Alright old man. Step out slowly.

The Sheriff doesn't look phased and doesn't flinch for a second. He puts his arms up and walks out slowly. Rose follows behind him with the gun to his head as they walk out from behind the counter. She looks around, trying to gather intel of her surroundings, observing through her visor.

SHERIFF

Not bad for a rookie you know. Finding your way here, taking out 13 on the way in.

He pauses and slowly turns around as he notices a sense of doubt on her face.

ROSE

13? That supposed to mean something? How do you know how I found my way?

SHERIFF

Oh come on Rose, can we stop pretending? I'm an ally. I'm here to help. Ghost reached out. The login? 40527? Yes, I got that message too.

Rose points the gun towards the computer on the table.

ROSE

Who are you?

SHERIFF

Let's take it easy huh? They call me THE SHERIFF. Now if you can put that down, maybe we can debrief you?

ROSE

You're agency?

She points the gun back up to him.

SHERIFF

I used to be, a long time ago. Let's just say Taylor, or as
you know him, Ghost, is like a godson to me.

They lock eyes.

SHERIFF (CONTD)

I'm only here to help you get your team back.

ROSE

What do you know about them? And how the fuck do
you know so much if you aren't in the fucking game?

SHERIFF

Allow me to show you..

He slowly steps over to the computer and hits a few keys on it. The
cashier counter goes into the wall and reveals a path with stairs.

SHERIFF

I'm old school honey. Go on.

She walks downs the spiral steps, leading her into an underground
bunker. The Sheriff, right behind her, steps to the side and pulls a lever
on the wall.

INT. TRUTH PIT. NIGHT

SHERIFF

Welcome to the Pit.

They walk through an arched doorway and into a Retro Ottoman-styled
Laboratory. As the lights power up, a large brass cylinder turns on with
neon green lights, switching on the smaller cylinders.

It all comes to life. The setting reveals a lair of technology behind it.

Rose looks around surprised. She has walked into a time capsule. Sheriff walks up to his computers and manually turns on all the switches.

SHERIFF

You wanted to know how I know what I know. But now I wanna know if you're interested to get Taylor and your crew back. No time to waste Rose. I need to know what happened? Why. Did. The. Op. Go South?

ROSE

How did you know it was an op?

She walks around looking at everything in detail while The Sheriff types into his screen. Multiple screens detach and unfold, revealing information about her operation.

SHERIFF

From this, which is what I picked up 3 minutes after I got Taylor's distress message. It looks like you'll were after something called 'The Black Box' and you were deep under cover.... How am I doing Rose?

ROSE

You seem to know a lot about something you're not part of anymore... Sheriff. I'd like to see Ghost's message now please.

SHERIFF

You do not walk into someone's house and demand to be fed. Not very polite, is it?

Rose turns around swiftly and grabs the Sheriff by the neck, pulling a knife on him. As she grabs him, she holds the tip of the blade at his eyeball.

She whispers into his ear.

ROSE

Tell me Sheriff, is it ok if I cook my own meal in your house? I'm done playing fucking games.

SHERIFF

Suit yourself. Dr. James Blackwood. Professor of Structural Informatics and Neuroscience.

Rose is taken aback and eases for a second, hearing the name of her father. As she drops her guard, the Sheriff reverses his position and pins Rose down. He pulls out a shotgun from under his table and points it at her. She tries to push him off and he pulls the shotgun and loads it.

SHERIFF

I knew your Dad, Rose. I know what happened to him. I'm sorry for your loss. Can we please stop this now? I'm on your side.

As a sign of good faith, he slowly drops the shotgun down and extends his arm out, offering to pick her up. She grabs his hand and gets up. Changing the setting on her visor, she takes off her helmet.

ROSE

My dad huh? Yeah he was something...but I'd like to bring my family back home please.

SHERIFF

Finally, music to my ears.

EXT. OFF THE COAST. DAWN

As the sun comes up, a cargo ship, in stealth grey, lays still. Through the burning halo of the sun on the horizon line, a black hawk helicopter descends towards the ship, which has a modified helipad in the centre. Containers surround the helipad to hide the landing site. The black hawk lands in as armed militants form a perimeter around the chopper.

EXT. CARGO SHIP DECK. DAWN

Agent Shaw steps out with armed security besides him. The CAPTAIN of the ship salutes him, greeting him as they head indoors.

INT. BLACK SITE CONTAINER. DAY

Range looks at Ghost with his hands zipped behind his back. Ghost shuffles his back to the wall and grabs onto a screw from a vent. He unscrews it half-way through, and slowly using the screw to cut free his zip tie, starts slicing it.

RANGE

There's only 10 people that knew about our operation. Someone has gone through a lot of trouble to keep us alive.

ANGEL

We don't even have the black box.

RANGE

But if they've kept us here, it means Rose has what they want.

GHOST

If she's smart, she'll meet an ally. I sent our drone coordinates to my old man's friend.

RANGE

Who?

Ghost shows Range his watch.

GHOST

Managed to send out our digits to someone special.

RANGE

Are you sure?

GHOST

He's practically family.

RANGE

He better be, because if by some miracle Rose made it out, and if you know her at all. She'll put him down in a second.

ANGEL

But if she did get the black box, I know homegirl. She's coming for us.

GHOST

Alright, time to get the fuck out. The container, what you thinking, shipping yard?

ANGEL

This is no shipyard. Shhhh....Quiet. Listen.

He gets up and helps Angel, who is stuck in the corner, free. As Angel frees Range, Ghost looks out of the window. Angel belts her leather pants and brushes off her violet hair. She puts her ear to the ground.

ANGEL

Listen to that. Low vibrations with a hollow echo. Those babies are engines. We are on a vessel.

Range, peaking through the glass, spots Agent Shaw alongside the Captain, walking towards them.

RANGE

Ghost check the valves, see if you can get us out of here.

Ghost climbs up and tries to unlock the hatch.

It's jammed.

He falls while trying to turn the wheel making a loud thud.

INT. WALKWAY CARGO SHIP. DAY.

SOLDIERS dressed in all black combat uniforms, armed with heavy firepower, walk ahead of Agent Shaw and the captain of the cargo ship.

The loud thud gets everyone's attention.

CAPTAIN

Check it out solider. NOW!

SOLIDER 1

Yes sir.

INT. BLACK SITE CONTAINER. DAY

Range sees the soldiers walking towards them.

RANGE

Incoming. Get down. Ghost!

He hand signals in military code -two soldiers- and points to his eyes, signalling he is watching them. Ghost and Angel acknowledge.

The door swings open. The solider walks in.

INT. WALKWAY CARGO SHIP. DAY

The Captain and Agent Shaw continue their walk through the walkways.

AGENT SHAW

Captain, I have an incoming package. Very important that needs to be kept safe here on your ship.

CAPTAIN

Absolutely Sir. I can show you the secure Lab downstairs. It's ready, just needs powering up.

AGENT SHAW

Good. We are going to need all the powering up.

INT. BLACK SITE CONTAINER. DAY

As the solider walks in, Range hides behind the door. He shuts the door, slamming it. He pulls the solider from his legs and knocks him in the head as he falls to the floor. Range jumps onto him in a rear-naked choke, putting him to sleep. He drags the body away.

INT. WALKWAY CARGO SHIP. DAY

The second soldier, standing not too far away, watches in concern. A deafening silence as his partner goes missing. He lifts his gun, pointing towards the door, and slowly walks forward.

INT. BLACK SITE CONTAINER. DAY

The soldier cautiously pushes open the door as he sees Angel and Ghost kneeling down with their hands tied behind their back. In search of his partner, he turns the corner looking behind the door.

Range shuts the door as Ghost sneaks up from behind, kicking and breaking the soldier's knee, grabbing his mouth to keep him silent. He takes out the soldier's knife and smoothly slices his throat.

GHOST

Shhhh. Easy there.

He wipes the blood on his own leg. Range picks up the radio.

RANGE

All clear with the prisoners. Just a leak Boss.

RADIO

Copy that Mikey. Get up to the deck now. We have a package coming in.

RANGE

Copy that Sir.

Angel looks at Range hearing that. She smiles. Ghost starts taking the soldier's clothes off him.

EXT. EAST INDIA COMPANY. DAY

A convoy with two bikes leading the motorcade, followed by two armoured SUVs, maintains tight distance as security detail speeds through the city. The Indian flag is posted in front of the Mercedes limousine - the centre of the armoured convoy. The city outside is dusted in the juxtaposition of social wealth classes; with slums on one side and skyscrapers on the other. A futuristic South-Asian setting crowded with people as life begins through the morning.

The convoy goes under the Metro, passing a huge billboard of 'Khan Industries Limited: GIO-Digital.' On the billboard is the CEO extraordinaire, JACKIE KHAN, 40, in a suit with a stylish sleek mask on him.

INT. MERCEDES LIMO KHAN. DAY

Jackie Khan is smartly dressed in a three-piece suit with his hair slicked back; he has a Gucci metal mask on that is see-through. He smiles as he looks at himself on the reflection of the building, talking to his assistant, LI ANN.

JACKIE KHAN

Li, make sure the Ambassador knows we are in support of his wife's charity please, get her a diamond ring too. And some sexy underwear. Hmmmmm those butt cheeks on her.

He bites his hand as he fantasises about the Ambassador's wife.

LI ANN

(Smiling sarcastically)

Of course Sir. I'll make sure of it. This is a transcript of your speech sir.

JACKIE KHAN

Hey, come on, you know it's just business.

LI ANN

I know, Sir.

INT. AUDITORIUM. DAY

An audience of 500 is seated in an auditorium. Everyone has stylish masks on, sporting the hashtag '# KHANGIO.' The main screen has Khan industries logo. It says, 'Khan Keynote.'

ANNOUNCER

Ladies and gentlemen, we have long awaited this - the future came to us because of this man. And once again he is here to help us live our dreams. The cure to human error. This is life reinvented. Please put your hands together for none other than the richest man in the world right now, but also the number 1 on the ladies list. To introduce to you, MR. JACKIE KHAN!

The audience erupts as they all get on their feet clapping and cheering all excited. The hip hop music intro kicks in as does the fire and lights show. Out walks Jackie Khan, waving to the audience.

JACKIE KHAN

Thank you. Thank you very much everyone. Namaste and Good morning. When I was a little kid, I used to be scared of the Dark, till one day I learned that darkness is nothing else but the absence of visible photons. It's a bit silly I'd say to be afraid of something that isn't even there.

Beat.

JACKIE KHAN

Would you agree?

AUDIENCE

YES!!

Jackie smiles as he walks across the stage and stops.

JACKIE KHAN

Would you be scared of me if you couldn't see me?

As the lights shut out, so does the power. Jackie disappears. The audience is shocked. He suddenly reappears in the back of the stands in between the audience and continues.

JACKIE KHAN

Or what if I told you, you could see me when you want.
Where you want.

He disappears again from in-between the audience and appears back on stage. Everyone is shocked. They all start clapping at the marvel of the trick.

JACKIE KHAN

Thank you..You see, one of the main causes of artistic decline in our society today is the separation of Art and Science. And so that got me thinking, what if we bridged that gap with something a bit more intellectual.

Beat.

JACKIE KHAN

Something with the ability to Interact exactly as it were to appear. No more darkness. Only light!

Suddenly on stage, appear five different versions of Jackie Khan. Each of him dressed exactly the same, but all walking in different directions on the stage, waving out to the audience and taking a bow.

The audience is losing their mind. They cannot believe their eyes.

JACKIE KHAN

Which is why my latest tech platform is called - I.I. which stands for Intellectually Interactive.

Jackie Khan walks out from behind the stage. The audience acknowledges the presence of the real Khan and stands up applauding.

JACKIE KHAN

Welcome to the future. Deception is the art of War, these are not simulations but calculations, our algorithm studies its subject and develops a virtual you. These are versions of me

(Pointing to his clones)

made by me, from me. YOU get to live different versions of your life, RIGHT NOW! Not in your dreams, not online only. Here in reality and all at no risk. Think about all our soldiers, the lives we can save. Haven't we sacrificed enough lives already?

A man from the audience gets up and shoots one of the clones of Mr. Khan in the head. The bullet goes right through him. It's a hologram.

JACKIE KHAN

No more darkness. Only Light!

ANNOUNCER

Ladies and Gentlemen give it up for Mr. Jackie KHANNNNN!

INT. MERCEDES LIMO KHAN. DAY

JACKIE KHAN

Do you think they bought it?

He watches a live stream of the whole event on his tablet.

JACKIE KHAN

I love the future. Those poor fans don't even realise they're cheering for a hologram.

The real Jackie Khan looks a bit anxious. He starts sweating a little bit. Li hands him a glass of water. He takes out his pen and unscrews the back of it. Pouring out cocaine into a small spoon, he takes a deep breath in, inhaling it all. He drinks the water in a single gulp.

Li, sitting opposite him, watches him with stone cold eyes. He looks at her and pauses, slowly extending his arm out asking her to take a bit.

She jumps onto him and starts kissing him. She snorts the ball of cocaine as Jackie rips her shirt and starts kissing her. She moans, enjoying him as he picks her up, and puts her on the floor of the car.

INT. TRUTH PIT. DAY

As the morning rays come through the window of Truth, the city is alive. Broken rays of light form lines, casting illuminating shadows onto the pit. The Sheriff is asleep on the chair. The screen in front of him has a notification: 'Triangulating beacon current location...'

The software keeps bouncing off different locations. Rose sets down an old school boom box. She hits the play button. 'Let It Be' by Labyrinth starts.

The Sheriff wakes up with a start. He hears Rose kicking the punching bag.

Montage: Of Rose training on the punching bag, and then on the mat, she practices rolling in an Aikido style. She then practices open hand combat techniques on a mannequin. The Sheriff observes her training as he sips his coffee, putting his legs up on his table.

His computer screen pops up with a notification. 'Last known beacon location.'

Rose hears the pop-up onscreen and stops.

SHERIFF

That's the closest we are going to get too.

ROSE

Let me guess? Chinatown?

SHERIFF

Well, you sure know your ink alright!

Rose turns and starts walking away.

ROSE

Find me a face, not a fucking district.

She sighs

ROSE (CONTD)

I ran with the Russians when I was younger, I know how C-town does business. It's a one-way transaction and they usually choose.

SHERIFF

The agency can't do their own dirty work now can they? There's just too much to go through here.

As he accesses the security camera feeds from Chinatown, Rose makes a face at him and nudges him away. She types a few lines of code, uploading photos of Range, Angel, and Ghost. The software uses the images to find a match. A few seconds later, a notification.

'No Matches'

Rose looks at the Sheriff as he smiles. Her patience is being tested. He takes a deep breath. She has a glint in her eye as she takes out a photo of Connor from the 'Irishmen' and uploads it. A few seconds later it comes up with a match.

ROSE

I know this son of a bitch has answers. Wait a second.

Rose zooms into the footage and sees a man in a Suit. She changes cameras and looks at other footage, then zooms in further. It's Agent Shaw.

FLASHBACK

INT. INTERPOL ACADEMY. DAY

A FEW YEARS AGO...

Twelve new RECRUITS stand in three rows. All of them are standing in attention as they are briefed by their officer, a younger Agent Shaw, parading in para-military uniform.

AGENT SHAW

If you all think you made the cut and the job's done, I'm here to tell you, you are wrong. What's the first thing we learn about war here at the Farm....Blackwood?

ROSE

A solider must follow orders, Sir!

AGENT SHAW

Wrong! The first thing we learn is Deception is the Art of War. Nothing is what it seems. Do you understand?

RECRUITS

(together)

YES SIR!

AGENT SHAW

What's the second thing we learn...Ricci?

He looks directly at Ghost.

GHOST

We never leave loose ends.

ROSE

(interrupting)

We never leave our own behind.

AGENT SHAW

That's right Agent Blackwood. Quick learner. And Mr. Ricci, sometimes we need loose ends to join the dots. It's knowing which ones to close and which ones to turn to our advantage.

END FLASHBACK

INT. TRUTH PIT. DAY

Rose looks at the screen.

SHERIFF

Care to share? Who's he?

ROSE

My CO. Agent Shaw. He trained us at the farm. He trained all of us.

SHERIFF

There they are. Look, they got moved into a freight truck. HK ports.

ROSE

(In thought)

HK Ports...hmmm

A beat.

ROSE

We need to find a way in.

SHERIFF

If you are thinking, what I think you are, you are crazy.

ROSE

If you think that you can think what I think, you must be off your meds old man.

Rose picks up her weapon and holsters it.

ROSE

Stay away from my business

EXT. CHINESE AMBASSADOR'S MANSION. DAY

The Motorcade of Jackie Khan comes to a stop in front of a beautifully maintained fountain and lawn that is surrounded by trees. In the background is an 18th-century Gothic marvel of architecture with a large arched entrance. A group of people await the arrival of Mr. Khan with gifts and flags to exchange.

Mr. Khan appears to be unfazed by the grand gestures and walks right up the red-carpet leaving Li Ann to walk behind him. She greets the people around and gets caught with festivities. She tries to keep up.

Jared walks out with the CHINESE AMBASSADOR as they greet each other.

JACKIE KHAN

Mr. Ambassador, it is such an honour.

CHINESE AMBASSADOR

The pleasure is all mine, Mr. Khan. Please...welcome to my house. Huan Ying.

JACKIE KHAN

Huan Ying...??

He looks over to Li Ann, confused.

LI ANN

It means to welcome...huan ying.

Jackie Khan smiles, then repeats the words.

JACKIE KHAN

Huan ying. Yes thank you. Che che.

INT. CHINESE AMBASSADOR'S MANSION. DAY

Jackie Khan completely ignores Jared standing right beside the Ambassador as Jared steps forward to shake hands. He is insulted and cringes. He follows behind Khan and the Ambassador as Khan makes dirty jokes and laughs away.

JACKIE KHAN

You know, the best happy ending massage I ever had was in Chinatown. HAHAHA. BTW where is Mrs. Chan, I haven't seen her in a while.

CHINESE AMBASSADOR

Haha, yes you have a funny sense of humour Mr. Khan. Unfortunately, she won't be able to make it tonight.

LI ANN

(In Mandarin)

I apologise on Mr. Khan's behalf, please excuse his words Mr. Ambassador.

CHINESE AMBASSADOR

(In Mandarin)

Don't worry. This fool doesn't realise what he just got himself into.

JACKIE KHAN

(In Mandarin)

A fool Am I Mr. Ambassador? Funny you say that. Last time I checked your wife wasn't with you at the Penthouse, right?

They step into the living area. Jared shuts the doors behind him, locking the entrance.

JARED

Mr. Khan, it's so nice of you to come all the way on such short notice. May I introduce myself, I will be in charge of your safety during your stay with us.

JACKIE KHAN

Hahaha I think you are mistaken. Mr?

JARED

Mr. Kusher, Jared Kusher.

JACKIE KHAN

And you are Head of Security? Because I have my own, thank you, as you can see my mini-Army outside.

CHINESE AMBASSADOR

Mr. Khan, I have a request from you. We need your help with a top-secret military project.

JACKIE KHAN

How can I help ambassador? But first. Can we get rid of your muscle here please? A bit weird..you know like a creep.

Khan tries to be funny, making faces while talking into Jared's face. Jared stares at him without blinking, looking right at him. Khan stands right in his face. He hears the click of a gun.

JARED

(Calmly whispering)

I tried to do this a bit differently you know. I was polite. But you just had to.

He turns swiftly in rage.

JARED

(Screaming)

SIT. Your ass down.

Khan is shocked and is trembling with anxiety.

JARED

LAST WARNING MOTHERFUCKER.

(In Khan's face)

In the name of everything that is dripped in holy and tripped in molly, if you don't get your brown ass down now-

JACKIE KHAN

Okay okay okay, let's all calm down, shall we?

He offers him a pill.

JARED

The fuck is this?

JACKIE KHAN

You said something about molly in there. I thought you could use some.

Jared puts the gun to Khan's head. And then turns to the ambassador.

JARED

(Pointing his gun downward)

You too Sushi...down

They both sit down on the couch with Li Ann standing still.

Jared is back to being calm.

JARED

(Mocking)

Welcome to Interpol. Huan ying motherfucker. Are you feeling home now? It's time to get this party started. Call in the team and tie them up.

Both Khan and the Ambassador are looking at each other confused.

Li Ann, stepping forward, pulls a needle from a hidden thigh sleeve, bending over Khan.

LI ANN

Sorry darling. It's just business.

She injects him while watching his face turn white in shock.

JACKIE KHAN

You?..You work for Interpol? But why...

He falls to sleep, unconscious. Li turns around and jumps onto Jared kissing him.

JARED

I love it when you get dirty with me. Fuck I've missed you.

The Chinese ambassador is still awake. Jared is wearing gloves. He points the gun at him and pulls the trigger.

JARED

I'm sorry ambassador, you have been transferred.

He hands Li the gun, who then puts it in the hands of Khan, getting his fingerprints on it.

INT. WALKWAY CARGO SHIP. DAY

Range and Ghost have worn the captured soldiers' uniforms. They stand guard with Angel in between, chained and handcuffed. They both have weapons on them. They slowly make their way looking over their shoulders. They reach a staircase. Range walks up, clearing a path. Angel and Ghost follow behind.

RANGE

Ghost I need you to find us a ride out of here. Meet you at the rendezvous point in 10mins. Ready? Set.

They both set their watches to a 10-minute countdown.

EXT. IRISHMEN OFFICE. DAY

A count down timer has 10 seconds on it. Rose hides and takes cover as she sets a charge on the door.

She speaks into her comms.

> ROSE
>
> Charges Set. I'm going in.

INT. TRUTH DELIVERY VAN. DAY

The Sheriff is inside the Van with a full system setup as he watches Rose's every move.

> SHERIFF
>
> 4 hostiles armed inside. One looks like he's counting money. And Connor. As you enter, 9 O'clock and 11 O'clock.

Rose reloads her gun and sets her visor to 'Combat Mode.' A large explosion sets off, blowing off the main door of the office on the main road.

INT. IRISHMEN OFFICE. DAY

Connor is sitting on a desk that is stacked full of money being counted by an elderly man in a bowtie. He pisses his pants after the explosion. The explosion has taken out two guards at the door. With the charges exploding, Rose comes crashing in from the side, using the explosion as decoy, and gets two perfect headshots of the other guards. She then starts open firing all through the office. The elderly man sits still in his chair, shivering, as bullets fly around him. The guards around him drop to the floor. Connor shuts his ears as he hides under his table.

Rose enters, open firing at everything, completely wrecking the place. All that's left is bullet holes in the wall. She drops her magazine from the gun and reloads as the silence takes over after the explosion.

ROSE

Long time Connor. Remember me? What was that? The boss always gets it all.....AA AAAA NO NO I wouldn't if I were you.

Rose turns to the old man who is trying to reach for the gun.

ROSE

You and I need to talk. And this time YOU are going to tell me exactly what I want to know.

The old man tries again to reach for the Gun. Rose shoots him in the head, execution style. Two to the chest and one to the head.

ROSE

Now it's just you and me fancy pants. Where is Shaw?

CONNOR

You know as well as I do, I give you that information and I'm a dead man.

ROSE

You don't and you're a dead man for sure. Your choice Connor.

She reloads her pistol and points it at him.

CONNOR

Ok ok ok..Stop. Wait, just wait ok. I don't know where he is, but we did deliver a package to the docks.

ROSE

Wrong answer, I already know that. Goodbye Connor.

CONNOR

STOP STOP PLEASE. I'll tell you. Wait. If I tell you though, will you let me go? Please..

ROSE

I don't think you're in a position to negotiate. But if you do, I promise not to kill you.

CONNOR

The briefcase, there's a phone in there. It's a secure line to Shaw, that's how he gets in touch.

Rose reaches for the briefcase and gets the phone out.

She sees the last dialled number on it. It says unknown. She looks at Connor in anger and swings her knife, stabbing his hand to the table. Blood gushes out of Connor's hand as he screams in pain.

ROSE

No more games Connor. Your time's up.

CONNOR

OK, OK! They're on a vessel. I have a guy on the inside. I'll get you the location.

ROSE

But first, do you know who this guy is?

INT. TRUTH DELIVERY VAN. DAY

Rose and the Sheriff start driving away from Connor's office as the police show up. They get away in the opposite direction.

SHERIFF

How did you know he was holding out?

ROSE

I spent 6 months undercover with that asshole. I know how he thinks. He always has leverage, but he likes to have ears everywhere, and the police - That would be you?

SHERIFF

Time for the king to get off his throne, don't you think?

Rose smiles. The Sheriff smiles back. Rose looks at her table in front of her. She has the location of the vessel locked in. She hits memories on her phone gallery and chooses 'family' to bring up her photo with her team on her device. Her eyes fill up. Rose looks outside as they drive though the scenic terrain.

ROSE

Hang in there guys. I'm coming for you.

She swipes to the left by mistake, revealing an intimate topless photo of Rose with another woman. She quickly turns her device off and clears her throat. Sheriff looks at her. She is looking away.

INT. ELECTRICAL ROOM CARGO SHIP. DAY

Range has disconnected wires running along the mainframe and has plugged a device in. Angel is keeping guard.

ANGEL

What are you doing?

RANGE

Letting Rose know we are alive. And buying us some time.

Range types and hits send.

INT. TRUTH DELIVERY VAN. DAY

As Rose looks at the vessel's location and reads data, her notification pops up.

'Only in the ocean are the valleys deeper still

Yet a war on land continues to break our will'

Rose smiles as she reads that.

                    ROSE

They are alive.

                    SHERIFF

How do you know?

                    ROSE

Because Range just told me so.

Rose writes the message again, only spacing four words in a line. She circles the last two words from the bottom upwards.

It reads:

                Our Will continues to war.

                Valleys deeper in the ocean.

                    ROSE

They're breaking free, but they have negative extraction.

                    SHERIFF

Guess things really have changed since I've left.

INT. CARGO SHIP BRIDGE. DAY

TWO OFFICERS report to the Captain.

                    OFFICER

Captain on the bridge.

                    XO OFFICER

Captain, you need to see this. We just picked up an open message outbound to a secure channel.

                    CAPTAIN

What's the message?

XO OFFICER

Only in the ocean are the valleys deeper still. Yet a war on land continues to break our will.

AGENT SHAW

Check the prisoner room now! They just sent a message that could mean anything. Captain we need to move to DEFCON 1.

CAPTAIN

Pardon me sir, but this is a stealth ship posing as a civilian vessel. We cannot just disappear off the radar.

AGENT SHAW

Captain. I'm not going to ask you again, this ship needs to be protected and the information on it. We cannot let anyone get on this ship, DO you understand?

CAPTAIN

XO, move to Defcon 1. Prepare to send out a statement that we had a technical error to the Port authority.

INT. ELECTRICAL ROOM CARGO SHIP. DAY

All the lights suddenly change and everything turns red.

CAPTAIN

This is the captain speaking. Everyone move to your stations, we are now at DEFCON 1. All personnel at your stations now.

Sirens start all around the ship as everyone is running to mind their post.

RANGE

And now we make our move. DEFCON 1. Nothing goes in or out over the radio.

Ghost enters the electrical room from the hatch above them. He pulls Angel up and gives Range the thumbs up.

GHOST

I got the south exit. Let's circle back to the Bridge.

RANGE

See you on the other side. Wakanda forever?

He winks.

GHOST

(In action)

For Wakanda

ANGEL

(Shutting the hatch)

Wakanda my ass, you need the fucking force

INT. TRUTH DELIVERY VAN. DAY

Rose looks at a marine radar on her tablet. She watches as everything remains still. She gets a notification: 'Incoming bound: Korea Town KT01.'

She sighs as her hopes come crashing. She hits 'refresh' multiple times.

ROSE

Gotchya!

INT. CHINESE AMBASSADOR'S MANSION. DAY

Jared lays a record on the Gramophone. As he hears the scratch of the record starting, he takes a long sip of his whiskey. The song 'Labradford' by Chris Johnson begins.

Montage:

An elderly man, 60s, with a thick white beard and long hair, handcuffed with chains on his ankles, slowly makes his way up the stairs from the dungeon below. Shackled and heavily guarded, his eyes adjust to the brightness as he looks around multiple guards, all heavily armed in suits, escorting this prisoner. In front of him, Jared and Li are waiting. Jared, sipping his whiskey, smiles.

EXT. HELIPAD CHINESE AMBASSADOR'S MANSION. DAY

The bearded shackled man is followed by Jackie Khan, both of them chained together. A heavy prisoner guard formation protects the prisoners as the wind from the helicopter pushes the leaves to fly around.

The door of the military helicopter opens with four Navy seals jumping out as they run towards the prisoners.

INT. NAVY HELICOPTER. DAY

The prisoners have their faces covered with ear protection and a chained metal mask. The handcuffs switch colour from red to white. The prisoners' masks turn white on the screen. As they inhale and breathe through, they lose head control, knocking them out.

The Seals look at each other. One of them hits a button on his table. It reads - 'Ketamine 5mg1sin.'

Jared watches the helicopter take off.

EXT. MARINE LIFE DOCKS. DAY

Rose looks through a sleek metal headset. She adjusts the scope buttons as she looks back at her tablet, moving the timeline on it till the Cargo ship disappears. She gets a coordinate lock and looks back through the scope.

EXT. BINOCULARS SCOPE. DAY

Rose can see the cargo vessel in the distance. As she scans the area, she spots the inbound helicopter heading in that direction.

EXT. MARINE LIFE DOCKS. DAY

A group of SOMALI FISHERMEN gather together as they have a party. They toast and have a laugh. Rose walks up to them and speaks in Somali.

ROSE

(In Somali)

How much to go fishing?

SOMALI LEADER

Keep walking white girl, ain't no fishing for you today.

ROSE

Either you name your price, or I can make an offer. Plata
O Plomo

SOMALI LEADER

Who the fuck you think you are, you little Chiquita
whore? Walk away or come suck my dick.

All his friends laugh as he ridicules Rose. She takes out a knife and
throws it towards the Somali leader, slicing his hand that is holding
the beer. His hand falls to ground and the bottle breaks. Blood sprays
everywhere.

He starts screaming and jumping around, spraying blood on everyone's
face. Rose hits a button that magnetises her knife and comes flying back
to her. She wipes it on her thigh and lifts it in the air to see her reflection.
She spots some blood and licks her finger to slowly rub it off. In her
reflection is a large muscular African male. A bullet goes flying from
behind Rose into the Somali Leader's head as he falls into the water.

Standing behind her is IDRIS, aka Big Fish, 30s, a perfectly ripped body
with gold chains and fancy glasses. He walks forward.

IDRIS

(Pointing to his people around)

They call me Big Fish. You...can call me when you want
to pay back for the man you just cost me.

ROSE

How about some guns, cash, toys, oh and how about a 1200ft cargo ship for your little collection here?

Idris smiles at her. He nods his head as he cleans his machete.

IDRIS

I like how you do business.

A beat.

They both drop their guards and smile warmly as they embrace each other.

IDRIS

(In Somali)

Load the ships, we got a whale to catch boys.

INT. BRIDGE OF CARGO SHIP. DAY

Range stealthily takes cover in-between the staircase with the bridge in sight. He looks at his device. It's counting down from: 00:08, 00:07...

INT. WALKWAY UPPER DECK CARGO SHIP. DAY

Ghost and Angel simultaneously walk-up behind two guards and slice their necks. They cover the guards' mouths as they cross sides, nodding towards each other. Ghost actions out to her to take opposite corners. He counts her down. 3...2..1.

INT. BRIDGE OF CARGO SHIP. DAY.

Range storms the bridge shooting two guards in the head and the XO on the wheel.

RANGE

DOWN!! NOW! GET DOWN ON THE GROUND.

Everyone starts panicking and falls to the floor.

RANGE

I wouldn't do that if I were you.

He points the gun to a FEMALE CREW MEMBER who is about to hit the alarm button. She reacts, being scared.

FEMALE CREW MEMBER

Please, I'm just a civilian please, let me go. I promise I won't do anything.

GHOST

Alpha?

RANGE

All clear.

Ghost and Angel come through inside as they scope around for possible threats, pointing their guns to each person on the floor.

RANGE

Where is your captain?

INT. WAR ROOM CARGO SHIP. DAY

The captain and Agent Shaw are sitting in a briefing as they are interrupted by an OFFICER.

OFFICER CARGO SHIP

Captain, I think you need to see this.

The officer turns on the live feed from the ship's deck, looking out to the ocean. They see about thirty dhow ships heading their way.

AGENT SHAW

What is that? Captain we have an incoming package. This vessel is to be fully secured. NOW!

CAPTAIN

Sergeant, Activate all artillery aboard. And reach out via comms telling them to keep away. I'm heading to the bridge.

Agent Shaw and the Captain exit the room in a rush.

INT. FISHING BOAT. DAY

Rose is standing next to Idris in a tightly spaced cabin as Idris yells out to his men.

IDRIS

(In Somali)

Shhh..quiet, move the rudder and let us drift in.

ROSE

This better work.

Rose walks out of the cabin and looks at the cargo vessel not too far from her.

EXT. FISHING BOAT. DAY

Rose is fully armoured and geared-up, set in Combat mode, with her Sniper in her hand. She sets it on the tip of the boat and lays down to get comfortable. She peaks through her scope.

EXT. SNIPER SCOPE. DAY.

Rose spots two armed guards patrolling the back of the ship. She can see them exchange laughs as they each light a cigarette.

INT. FISHING BOAT. DAY

Idris instructs his man to speed up a little bit. As they get closer to the cargo ship, the boat hits a wave.

EXT. SNIPER SCOPE. DAY

Rose loses aim as the wave throws her off a bit. She adjusts herself again and takes a deep breath in. As the men hug each other to say goodbye, Rose fires the shot.

EXT. BULLET TIME. DAY

The bullet leaves the gun as time slows down. Piercing through the air and heading straight for the Cargo ship. The bullet splits into two parts, with a chained connector between them, like a staple pin. As it hits, both men are struck in the neck together, stapling their necks to the ground. They both bleed instantly, falling down and dead.

INT. FISHING BOAT. DAY

IDRIS

Impressive.

Rose smiles as she folds her gun into two, placing it on her back, as she removes a harpoon out.

EXT. TRUTH VAN. DAY

The Sheriff looks at the satellite images and then spots on his radar something moving in fast.

SHERIFF

Rose, the Helio will touch down in 2mins.

INT. WALKWAY UPPER DECK CARGO SHIP. DAY

Jared and the Captain make their way towards the bridge. As they enter and realise everyone is missing, Ghost and Angel put a gun to their heads.

INT. BRIDGE OF CARGO SHIP. DAY

RANGE

It's been a while SIR! Or should I say Double Agent Shaw.

AGENT SHAW

You think I was a double agent? You have no idea what you're dealing with.

RADIO ON BRIDGE

Captain, come in captain...No response from the bridge and these pirates are getting closer Sir.

AGENT SHAW

Hanging around with pirates now Ford? Didn't see you for the money type.

RANGE

Where is Rose? And what have you'll done with her.

RADIO ON BRIDGE

Sir, helio is touching down now. Package will be moved to prison level.

RANGE

Package? Agency package?

SHAW

That's none of your business, just like being here. You are out of your depths soldier.

Shaw adjusts his suit and tie as he puts on his sunglasses.

ANGEL

Where the fuck is Rose? NOW asshole.

She hits him in the face.

INT. LOWER DECK CARGO SHIP. DAY

Rose climbs onto the ledge and draws her shotgun. She scopes the place out and slowly walks through the corridors. The pipes have steam coming out. It's awfully silent. She hears footsteps and a sudden loud clunk.

Rose taps her earpiece and turns it off as she kneels down to set her gun on the floor. She takes off her shoes and her jacket, slowly folding the jacket, neatly placing it next to her shoes. She puts her headphones perfectly in the centre of her jacket, pulling out a silver metal cube. She holds the cube and touches it on her third eye, activating it to transform and expand into a shiny metal visor. She draws her knife.

Rose kneels down and puts her gun besides her. She removes her earpiece and draws her knife. She puts on her headphones.

ROSE

Alexa, play it.

Alexa plays 'Wise Enough' by Lamb. Rose smiles. As a guard appears, she wall rides, barefoot, activating her magnetic socks. She jumps to take his back while smoothly slicing his throat. Another two soldiers come around the corner, firing at her. She uses the guard as a shield. Running towards them, she climbs onto the guard, flying on top of him. As she draws her pistol to shoot two perfect head shots, she comes crashing to her side as all three bodies drop.

From behind come three soldiers, Rose springs up, rolling on the floor and shooting all three of them in the head. She gets up and reloads.

EXT. CARGO SHIP DECK. DAY

Rose walks out and swiftly turns the corners to check for threats. She walks ahead, pointing the gun upwards as she scans the staircase. She cautiously climbs, and as she steps out, six soldiers start firing at her. She takes cover and pulls out a grenade from her vest. She pulls the pin and throws it over her head. As the grenade detonates, she times her run and draws her weapon, firing three perfect shots taking out the three left in destruction. Rose walks away, watching the remaining burn in the aftermath of the explosion.

INT. BRIDGE OF CARGO SHIP. DAY

The Captain and Agent Shaw are kneeling down. Range is standing above him. Angel has a gun to their head.

AGENT SHAW

You see Ford, what's the first thing you were taught at the farm? Deception is the art of war.

Range looks at Shaw, he is smiling and gloating. He immediately runs to the systems and turns on the screen. He looks into the feeds and can see Rose. The screen says. 'Transmitting Live. Coordinates. 45.56788 23.77896.'

RANGE

You knew...you knew she would come for us. You used her as bait. SON OF A BITCH. I'M GOING TO KILL YOU!

AGENT SHAW

I told you, I only take orders just like you. In the end, Ford, we are all pawns on a chessboard.

EXT. HELIPAD CARGO SHIP. DAY.

From the helicopter step out four Navy seals as two others help the prisoners to step down. The metal masks open vents for their eyes and nose as the soldier changes the mode on his device to Transportation. The masks layer back across their face in sectors. As the sunlight pierces through into their eyes, they are escorted into the deck area.

INT. BRIDGE OF CARGO SHIP. DAY

Rose walks into the bridge area. It's empty. She is suddenly surrounded by twenty soldiers, all pointing lasers at her. It's over.

Fuming with rage, she reluctantly raises her hands after gradually dropping her weapons on the floor.

The prisoners enter with Agent Shaw, who steps forward. Rose looks at the prisoners and her face drops. It's her father, DR. BLACKWOOD, with Jackie Khan.

                              ROSE

DAD?

                         DR. BLACKWOOD

Hey kiddo. Long time.

                          AGENT SHAW

My brother sacrificed himself for this fucking family reunion. So it better be worth it.

Agent Shaw steps forward and uses the rear end of his gun to hit Rose in the face.

INT. ISLAND PRISON. NIGHT.

The crackle of thunder and lightning frightens Rose, waking her up. She holds her nose in pain and slowly shuts her eyes in anguish. She is bruised and slowly touches her face.

She looks to the other corner of the prison. In another cage is her father, and next to him, Jackie Khan. They are both asleep. She looks at them in despair. A tear drops from her eye as she turns to look outside.

EXT. ISLAND PRISON. NIGHT

In the deep forest, the wolves howl into a silent night as the moon hides behind the clouds. The thick jungle forms a silhouette of shapes. The rain comes down heavier and the sounds of thunder take over. She is trapped.

End of Pilot Episode.

Author

Uzair Merchant is the author of Black Rose, a Sci-Fi Show, built from the future. An fully interactive world built with NFT's and a Game that has recently launched its soundtrack, STARDUST. Black Rose is a part of the KREATIV UNIVERSE, produced by The Kreativ Lab by KRi8. The Lab's single aim is to create an avenue where art and artists can fluently express themselves, collaborate, and never lose their rights to their work.

With over 12 years in film business internationally as an 'ARTIST', Uzair has worked on various projects, including Star Trek Beyond, Fast and Furious 7, Skyfall, Deadpool 2, Superman and Lois. Most recently, he has production designed the first ever Hollywood film made in the UAE, 'The Misfits' by Renny Harlin (Die Hard 2, Cliffhanger) starring Pierce Brosnan and Jamie Chung.

A Kreativ explorer, Uzair takes on roles of a Production designer, writer, director & producer and has also designed for the world's largest cultural theme parks – Global Village in Dubai for over 6 years, winning the best pavilion award. His last short film "Chasing lines," (all shot on the iPhone) has won him 14 International awards from Los Angeles Film Award, New York Film Awards and, many more international festivals and currently streams on Amazon Prime and on all Sofy.tv platforms.

An alumnus of Nottingham Trent and the New York Film Academy, "Uzi" is a product of the world; with Indian roots, he's lived between Dubai, London, New York and is a resident of Vancouver. But it's not all lights, camera, and action...Music and Martial arts make up the other sides to who he is. He holds a 3rd Degree Black Belt in Shorin Ryu Seibukan Karate and strongly believes in Cosmic Creativity. The inner journey to the outer world.

CPSIA information can be obtained
at www.ICGtesting.com
Printed in the USA
LVHW070020301121
704793LV00001B/1